this book belongs to _____

dick bruna

the apple

Tate Publishing

there was a big red apple

in the green grass on the ground

the apple wept because he was

just an apple, rosy and round

why do you cry? asked the rooster

who stood on the tower up high

he spun when the wind blew hard

showing the way against the sky

oh rooster, see that beetle there

she is tiny but can walk

but an apple has no legs at all,

only a leaf and a stalk

of course I know the sun is bright

the leaves are green, the sky is blue

but I shall never have the chance

to see what all the people do

I'll help you, called the rooster

and listen, to what he said:

I'll pick you up tonight

when everyone's in bed

so down from the tower he flew

once the sky had turned quite black

and scooped up the rosy apple

who sat on the rooster's back

apple, take a look above you

there's a lovely butterfly

see its wings and glowing colours

as the creature flutters by

now here's a house where people live -

a door through which they go inside

and there's a window in the house

so shall we have a look, he cried

they peeped together through the window

what the apple saw was this

a bunch of grapes, all fat and purple

lying on a nice white dish

a fork and spoon lay on a table

on a cloth of coloured squares

and a sharp knife lay in between them -

with knives you must take great care!

listen, apple, we should hurry

it really is time for us to go

I must be back on the tower

before everyone wakes tomorrow

the apple was back on the ground

when the people woke at last

he shouted to his friend with joy

thanks rooster, we had a blast!

Other Dick Bruna books available from Tate Publishing:

I can count 2012
miffy the artist 2008
my vest is white 2012
on my scooter 2013
round, square, triangle 2012
the school 2013

Published 2013 by order of the Tate Trustees
by Tate Publishing, a division of Tate Enterprises Ltd,
Millbank, London SW1P 4RG
www.tate.org.uk/publishing

Based on the original translation © copyright Patricia Crampton, 1995
This edition © Tate 2013

Original edition: *de appel*
Original text Dick Bruna © copyright Mercis Publishing bv, 1959
Illustrations Dick Bruna © copyright Mercis bv, 1959
Publication licensed by Mercis Publishing bv, Amsterdam
Printed by Sachsendruck Plauen GmbH, Germany
All rights reserved.

A catalogue record for this book is available from the British Library
ISBN 978 1 84976 214 4

Distributed in the United States and Canada by ABRAMS, New York
Library of Congress Control Number: applied for